MEL BAY

GOSPEL FLATPICKING GUITAR
MADE EASY

BY WILLIAM BAY

CD Contents

1. Tuning Note [1:39]
2. All The Way My Savior Leads Me [0:50]
3. All The Way My Savior Leads Me (backup only) [0:50]
4. Angel Band [1:07]
5. Angel Band (backup only) [1:06]
6. Blessed be the Name [0:47]
7. Blessed be the Name (backup only) [0:47]
8. Hallelujah, We Shall Rise [0:39]
9. Hallelujah, We Shall Rise (backup only) [0:39]
10. Hold to God's Unchanging Hand [0:44]
11. Hold to God's Unchanging Hand (backup only) [0:44]
12. I Feel Like Traveling On [0:36]
13. I Feel Like Traveling On (backup only) [0:35]
14. I Have Found the Way [0:39]
15. I Have Found the Way (backup only) [0:39]
16. In the Garden [0:54]
17. In the Garden (backup only) [0:53]
18. Just Over in the Gloryland [0:48]
19. Just Over in the Gloryland (backup only) [0:49]
20. Life's Railway to Heaven [1:02]
21. Life's Railway to Heaven (backup only) [1:01]
22. The Church in the Wildwood [0:44]
23. The Church in the Wildwood (backup only) [0:44]
24. The Unclouded Day [0:42]
25. The Unclouded Day (backup only) [0:42]
26. 'Tis so Sweet [0:53]
27. 'Tis so Sweet (backup only) [0:53]
28. Where the Soul Never Dies [0:34]
29. Where the Soul Never Dies (backup only) [0:32]
30. I Will Live for Him [0:28]
31. I Will Live for Him (backup only) [0:27]

1 2 3 4 5 6 7 8 9 0

Visit us on the Web at www.melbay.com — E-mail us at email@melbay.com

Table of Contents

Tablature 3

All The Way My Savior Leads Me 4

Angel Band...6

Blessed be The Name...8

Hallelujah, We Shall Rise 10

Hold to God's Unchanging Hand...12

I Feel Like Traveling On 14

I Have Found the Way 16

In the Garden 18

Just Over in the Gloryland...20

Life's Railway to Heaven...22

The Church in the Wildwood...24

The Unclouded Day 26

'Tis so Sweet 28

Where the Soul Never Dies 30

I Will Live for Him 32

Chords Used

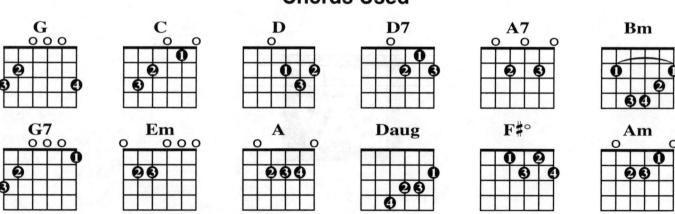

Tablature

Another way of writing guitar music is called *tablature*. The six horizontal lines represent the strings on a guitar. The top line is the first string. The other strings are represented by the lines in descending order as shown below.

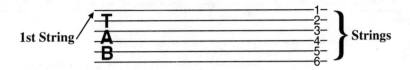

A number on a line indicates in which fret to place a left-hand finger.

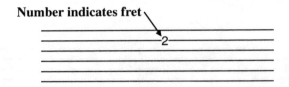

In the example below, the finger would be placed on the first string in the third fret.

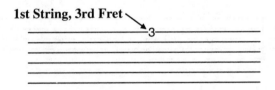

If two or more numbers are written on top of one another, play the strings at the same time.

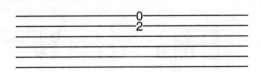

All the Way My Savior Leads Me

Tracks #2 & #3 (backup only)

1. All the way my Savior leads me; What have I to ask beside?
   Can I doubt His tender mercy? Who through life has been my guide?
   Heavenly peace, divinest comfort, Here by faith in Him to dwell!
   For I know whate'er befall me, Jesus doeth all things well;
   For I know whate'er befall me, Jesus doeth all things well.

2. All the way my Savior leads me, Cheers each winding path I tread,
   Gives me grace for every trial, Feeds me with the living bread.
   Thou my weary steps may falter, and my soul a thirst may be,
   Gushing from the rock before me, Lo! A spring of joy I see;
   Gushing from the rock before me, Lo! A spring of joy I see.

3. All the way my Savior leads me; O the fullness of His love!
   Perfect rest to me is promised, in my Father's house above.
   When my spirit, clothed immortal, wings its flight to realms of day,
   This my song through endless ages: Jesus led me all the way;
   This my song through endless ages: Jesus led me all the way.

Angel Band

Tracks #4 & #5 (backup only)

1. My latest sun is sinking fast,
   My race is nearly run.
   My strongest trials now are past,
   My triumph is begun.

Chorus

   Oh come, angel band, Come and around me stand,
   Oh bear me away on your snow white wings, to my immortal home,
   Oh bear me away on your snow white wings, to my immortal home.

2. Oh bear my longing heart to Him
   Who bled and died for me,
   Whose blood now cleanses from all sin
   And gives me victory.

Chorus

3. I've almost gained my heavenly home
   My spirit loudly sings,
   The holy ones, behold they come!
   I hear the noise of wings!

Chorus

Blessed Be the Name

1. Blessed be the name, Blessed be the name,
   Blessed be the name of the Lord.
   Blessed be the name, Blessed be the name, Blessed be the name of the Lord.

2. Worthy is the name,

3. Holy is the name,

4. Jesus is the name,

Hallelujah, We Shall Rise

Chorus

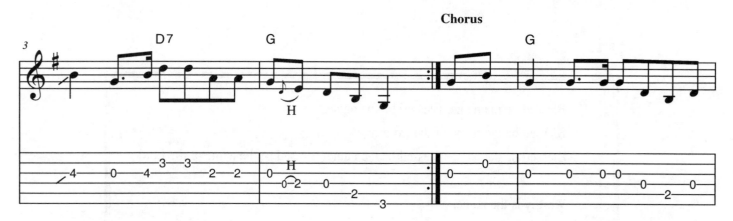

1. In the resurrection morning, When the trump of God shall sound,
   We shall rise, hallelujah! We shall rise,
   Then the saints will come rejoicing, And no tears will e'er be found,
   We shall rise, hallelujah! We shall rise,

Chorus

   We shall rise, hallelujah! We shall rise, Amen! We shall rise, hallelujah!
   In the resurrection morning, When death's prison bars are broken,
   We shall rise, hallelujah! We shall rise.

2. In the resurrection morning, What a meeting it will be,
   We shall rise, hallelujah! We shall rise,
   When our fathers and our mothers, And our loved ones we shall see,
   We shall rise, hallelujah! We shall rise,

Chorus

3. In the resurrection morning, Blessed thought it is to me,
   We shall rise, hallelujah! We shall rise,
   I shall see my blessed Savior, Who so freely died for me,
   We shall rise, hallelujah! We shall rise,

Chorus

Hold to God's Unchanging Hand

 Tracks #10 & #11 (backup only)

1. Time is filled with swift transition,
   Naught of earth unmoved can stand,
   Build your hopes on things eternal,
   Hold to God's unchanging hand.

Chorus

   Hold (to His hand) to God's unchanging hand
   Hold (to His hand) to God's unchanging hand
   Build your hopes on things eternal,
   Hold to God's unchanging hand

2. Trust in Him who will not leave you,
   Whatsoever years may bring,
   If by earthly friends forsaken,
   Still more closely to Him cling.

Chorus

3. Covet not this world's vain riches,
   That so rapidly decay,
   Seek to gain the heavenly treasures,
   They will never pass away.

Chorus

4. When your journey is completed,
   If to God you have been true,
   Fair and bright the home in glory,
   Your enraptured soul will view

Chorus

I Feel Like Traveling On

 Tracks #12 & #13 (backup only)

1. My heav'nly home is bright and fair,
   I feel like traveling on,
   No pain, no death can enter there,
   I feel like traveling on,

Chorus

   Yes, I feel like traveling on, I feel like traveling on,
   My heav'nly home is bright and fair, I feel like traveling on.

2. Its glit'ring towers the sun outshine,
   I feel like traveling on,
   That heav'nly mansion shall be mine,
   I feel like traveling on.

Chorus

3. Let others seek a home below,
   I feel like traveling on,
   Which flames devour, or waves o'er flow,
   I feel like traveling on.

Chorus

4. Be mine and happier lot to own,
   I feel like traveling on,
   A heav'nly mansion near the throne,
   I feel like traveling on.

Chorus

5. The Lord has been so good to me,
   I feel like traveling on,
   Until that blessed home I see,
   I feel like traveling on.

Chorus

I Have Found the Way

 Tracks #14 & #15 (backup only)

16

1. I have found the way that leads to endless day,
    Yonder in glory land,
    And the road is bright, For Jesus is the light,
    And I hold His guiding hand.

Chorus

    I have found the way, I have found the way,
    Glory hallelujah, I have found the way.

2. I will never fear,
    While Jesus is so near,
    I will bravely meet the foe,
    Happy song I'll sing,
    In honor to the King,
    And to glory onward go.

Chorus

3. To the journey's end,
    Led by a faithful Friend,
    Nevermore is sin to roam,
    By the way called straight,
    I'll reach the golden gate,
    Of the soul's eternal home

Chorus

In the Garden

1. I come to the garden alone while the dew is still on the roses,
   and the voice I hear falling on my ear, the Son of God discloses.

Chorus

   And he walks with me, and he talks with me, and he tells me I am his own;
   And the joy we share as we tarry there, none other has ever known.

2. He speaks, and the sound of his voice is so sweet the birds hush their singing,
   And the melody that he gave to me within my heart is ringing.

Chorus

3. I'd stay in the garden with him though the night around me be falling,
   But he bids me go; through the voice of woe his voice to me is calling.

Chorus

Just over in the Gloryland

Tracks #18 & #19 (backup only)

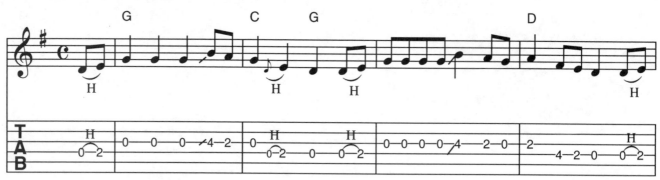

Chorus

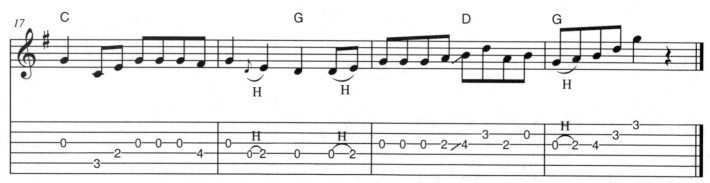

1. I've a home prepared where the saints abide,
   Just over in the gloryland.
   And I long to be by my Savior's side,
   Just over in the gloryland.

Chorus

   Just over in the gloryland, I'll join the happy angel band.
   Just over in the gloryland
   Just over in the gloryland, There with the mighty host I'll stand,
   Just over in the gloryland.

2. I am on my way to those mansions fair
   Just over in the gloryland,
   There to sing God's praise and his glory share
   Just over in the gloryland.

Chorus

3. What a joyful thought that my Lord I'll see
   Just over in the gloryland,
   And with kindred saved there forever be
   Just over in the gloryland.

Chorus

4. With the bloodwashed throng I will shout and sing
   Just over in the gloryland,
   Glad hosannas to Christ, the Lord and King,
   Just over in the gloryland.

Chorus

Life's Railway to Heaven

Tracks #20 & #21 (backup only)

1. Life is like a mountain railroad, with an engineer that's brave,
    We must make the run successful from the cradle to the grave;
    Watch the curves, the fills, the tunnel, never falter, never fail,
    Keep your hand upon the throttle and your eye upon the rail.

Chorus
    Blessed Savior, thou will guide us 'til we reach the blissful shore,
    Where the angels wait to join us in thy praise for evermore.

2. As you roll up the grade of trial, you will cross the bridge of strife,
    See that Christ is your conductor on the lightning train of life;
    Always mindful of obstruction, do your duty, never fail,
    Keep your hand upon the throttle and your eye upon the rail.

Chorus

3. As you roll across the trestle look for storm or wind and rain,
    On a curve or fill or trestle they will always ditch your train;
    Put your trust alone in Jesus, never falter, never fail,
    Keep your hand upon the throttle and your eye upon the rail.

Chorus

4. As you roll across the trestle, spanning Jordan's swelling tide,
    You behold the union depot into which your train will glide;
    There you'll meet the superintendent, God the Father, God the Son,
    With a hearty joyous plaudit, weary pilgrim, welcome home.

Chorus

The Church in the Wildwood

Tracks #22 & #23 (backup only)

1. There's a church in the vale by the wildwood,
   No lovelier spot in the dale,
   No place is so dear to my childhood
   As the little brown church in the vale.

Chorus

   Come to the church in the wildwood,
   Oh, come to the church in the vale,
   No spot is so dear to my childhood
   As the little brown church in the vale.

2. Oh, come to the church in the wildwood
   To the trees where the wild flowers bloom,
   Where the parting hymn will be chanted
   We will weep by the side of the tomb.

Chorus

3. How sweet on a clear Sabbath morning
   To list to the clear ringing bell,
   Its tones so sweetly are calling
   Oh, come to the church in the vale.

Chorus

4. From the church in the vale by the wildwood
   When day fades away into night,
   I would fain from this spot of my childhood
   Wing my way to the mansions of light.

Chorus

The Unclouded Day

Tracks #24 & #25 (backup only)

1. Oh they tell me of a home far beyond the skies,
    Oh they tell me of a home far away,
    Oh they tell me of a home
    where no storm clouds rise,
    Oh they tell me of an unclouded day.

Chorus
    Oh the land of cloudless day,
    Oh the land of an unclouded sky.
    Oh they tell me of a home
    where no storm clouds rise,
    Oh they tell me of an unclouded day.

2. Oh they tell me of a home
    where my friends have gone
    Oh they tell me of that land far away
    Where the tree of life in eternal bloom
    Sheds its fragrance through the unclouded day.

Chorus

3. Oh they tell me of a King in His beauty there
    And they tell me of that land far away
    Where the tree of life in eternal bloom
    In the city that is made of gold.

Chorus

4. Oh they tell me that He smiles
    on His children there
    And His smile drives their sorrows all away
    And they tell me that no tears ever come again
    In that lovely land of unclouded day.

Chorus

'Tis So Sweet

Tracks #26 & #27 (backup only)

1. 'Tis so sweet to trust in Jesus, and to take Him at His word;
   Just to rest upon His promise, And to know, "Thus saith the Lord."

Chorus

   Jesus, Jesus, how I trust Him! How I've proved Him o'er and o'er!
   Jesus, Jesus, precious Jesus! O for grace to trust Him more!

2. O how sweet to trust in Jesus, Just to trust His cleansing blood;
   And in simple faith to plunge me Neath the healing, cleansing blood!

Chorus

3. Yes 'tis sweet to trust in Jesus, Just from sin and self to cease;
   Just from Jesus simply taking Life and rest, and joy and peace.

Chorus

Where the Soul Never Dies

1. To Cannan's land I'm on my way
   Where the soul never dies.
   My darkest night will turn to day
   Where the soul never dies

Chorus
   No sad farewell,
   No tear dimmed eyes,
   Where all is love
   And the soul never dies

2. My life will end in deathless sleep,
   Where the soul never dies.
   And everlasting joys I'll reap,
   Where the soul never dies.

Chorus

3. I'm on my way to that fair land,
   Where the soul never dies.
   Where there will be no parting hand,
   Where the soul never dies.

Chorus

4. A rose is blooming there for me,
   Where the soul never dies.
   And I will spend eternity,
   Where the soul never dies.

Chorus

5. A love light beams across the foam,
   Where the soul never dies.
   It shines to light the shores of home,
   Where the soul never dies.

Chorus

I Will Live for Him

Tracks #30 & #31 (backup only)

1. My life, my love, I give to thee, Thou Lamb of God, who died for me;
   Oh may I ever faithful be, My Savior and my God!

2. O Thou who died on Calvary, To save my soul and make me free,
   I'll consecrate my life to Thee, My Savior and my God!

3. I'll live for Him who died for me, How happy then my life shall be!
   I'll live for Him who died for me, My Savior and my God!